To Alexandra, a loving friend and daughter   KH
To John and Pauline Craig   HC

Published by Pleasant Company Publications
© 2001 HIT Entertainment PLC
Text copyright © 1987 by Katharine Holabird
Illustrations copyright © 1987 by Helen Craig

Visit our Web sites at **americangirl.com** and **angelinaballerina.com**

Printed in Italy.
01 02 03 04 05 06 07 LEGO 10 9 8 7 6 5 4 3

Library of Congress Cataloging-in-Publication Data
Craig, Helen.
Angelina and Alice / illustrations by Helen Craig; story by Katharine Holabird.
p. cm.
Summary: Angelina and her best friend Alice discover the
importance of teamwork when their acrobatics are the hit
of the gymnastics show at the village fair.
ISBN 1-58485-130-9
[1. Friendship—Fiction. 2. Gymnastics—Fiction. 3. Mice—Fiction.]
I. Holabird, Katharine. II. Title.

PZ7.C84418 Aj 2001
[E]—dc21   00-041660

Angelina and Alice

Story by **Katharine Holabird** Illustrations by **Helen Craig**

PLEASANT
COMPANY
PUBLICATIONS™

Angelina jumped for joy the day Alice came to school.
Alice loved to dance and do gymnastics, and she was
good at all the same things as Angelina. They quickly
became close friends and were always together. At breaks
they skipped rope and did cartwheels round and round
the playground.

They loved to see who could hang upside down longest on the trapeze bar without wiggling, swing highest on the swings, or do the most somersaults in the air.

Angelina was good at cartwheels and could
even do the splits, but Alice could do
a perfect handstand with her toes
pointed straight in the air and
never lose her balance.

Angelina always fell over when she tried to do a handstand, which was embarrassing, especially on the playground.

One day Angelina fell right on her bottom, and the older children pointed at her and laughed. One of them giggled and said, "Look at Angelina Tumbelina!" Another whispered to Alice, and then…

…something awful happened. Alice giggled too and
ran off to play with the older children while Angelina
sat behind the swings and cried.

The next day was worse. They were all saying "Angelina Tumbelina!" on the playground, and Angelina couldn't find Alice anywhere. Angelina couldn't concentrate at school and made lots of mistakes in her spelling. She couldn't eat her sandwiches at lunch either, and by the time the class was lining up for gym, Angelina felt so sick she wished she could go home.

Mr. Hopper, the gym teacher, blew his whistle for silence and said, "You've all worked so hard at your gymnastics over the year that we are going to do a show for the village festival. Everyone needs to find a partner and start practicing now."

Angelina looked at the floor. Who could she ask? She was afraid nobody would be her partner. A big tear rolled down her nose.

Then she felt a tap on her shoulder. It was Alice!
"Will you be my partner, please?" Alice asked.

All that afternoon Angelina and
Alice worked on handstands in the
gymnasium. "Just keep your head
down and line up your tail with the
tip of your nose," Alice said patiently.
"That always helps me to stay up
straight longer." Alice was a good
teacher, and soon Angelina could do
a handstand without falling at all.

Mr. Hopper taught them how to swing in a beautiful circle over the bar and how to actually fly through the air and land neatly balanced on the mat.

He taught them to work with the rings and on the bars

and to do rhythmic gymnastics with colored ribbons.

Finally, Mr. Hopper showed them a
terrific balancing trick they could
do for the show.

The day of the village festival was
bright and beautiful.

TODAY
A DISPLAY
OF
GYMNASTICS
BY THE
CHILDREN
OF
MOUSLE SCHOOL

The gymnastics class did a wonderful display at the village festival with high jumps, back flips, and balancing on the bars. When Angelina and Alice did their balancing act together, even the older children were impressed. "Wow!" they said. "How did you learn to do those amazing tricks?"

PIN THE TAIL ON THE CAT & WIN A PRIZE!

After the show, Mr. Hopper smiled and said, "That was really good teamwork!"

Alice and Angelina grinned back. "That's because we're such good friends," they said together.

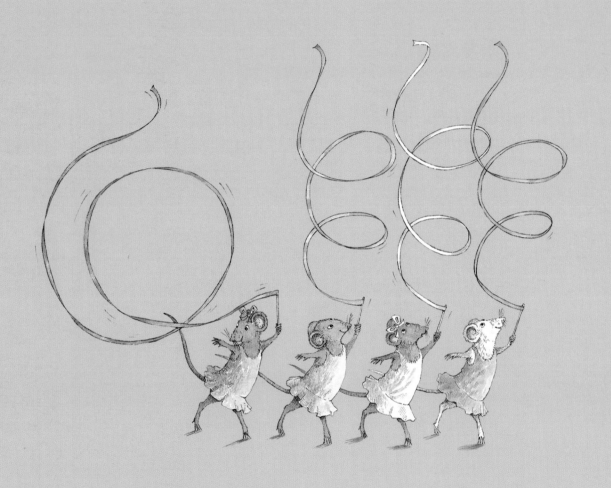

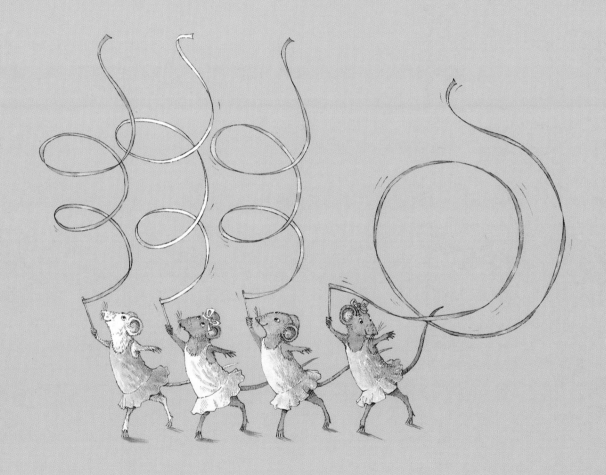

A free catalogue for your little ballerina!

If you've fallen in love with Angelina Ballerina,™ you'll love the American Girl catalogue. Angelina's world comes to life in a line of charming playthings and girl-sized clothes that complement her beautiful books. You'll also discover Bitty Baby,® a precious baby doll with her own adorable clothes and accessories.

To receive your free catalogue, return this card, visit our Web site at **americangirl.com**, or call **1-800-845-0005**.

Send me a catalogue:

Name

Address

City   State   Zip

My child's birth date: _____ / _____ / _____   86945i
                        month   day   year

Send my friend a catalogue:

Name

Address

City   State   Zip

                                                86947i

American Girl™

PO BOX 620497
MIDDLETON WI 53562-0497